My Life So Far

by

____

Formatted by

Gimmicky Pseudonym

Copyright © 2018 Gimmicky Pseudonym

Cover image by Jeremy Bishop at Unsplash

Author: Pseudonym, Gimmicky

ISBN: 978-0-6481463-3-9

Dedication:

CHAPTER ONE

13

ACKNOWLEDGEMENTS

I'd like to thank Gimmicky Pseudonym for creating this book
to house my writing talent

OTHER BOOKS IN THE BLANK BOOK SERIES.

The Girl in the Title

Summer Beach

Silhouette of a Man

Not Lost in Space But Still in a Lot of Trouble

Journey to a Destination

My Life So Far

Fairy Tale